To my Dad, for telling me the story and inspiring my imagination with silliness
for as long as I can remember.

The
Ooch~Me~Noodle
Bird

Dear Eilidh,

Enjoy reading and create a beautiful world.

Victoria Shaw

One afternoon when I was young, I walked with Grandpa to the park. The sun was shining, children and animals played on the grass, and the sound of laughter was all around. In shadowy bushes in a far corner, I spied a bright little eye looking back at me – a bird. I looked around a while and asked,

"Grandpa, why are all birds the same color? Dogs are brown, black, red and white, and all the other animals too. Even people come in many colors, but why are all the birds brown?"
"Well", he replied in a very sad voice, "let me tell you a story..."

3

Once, a very long long time ago
There were millions of birds in the world –
Blue birds and red birds and green birds and black birds,
Every color, or so I am told.
Birds came in ones or twos or threes,
Birds lived down low and birds lived in trees.

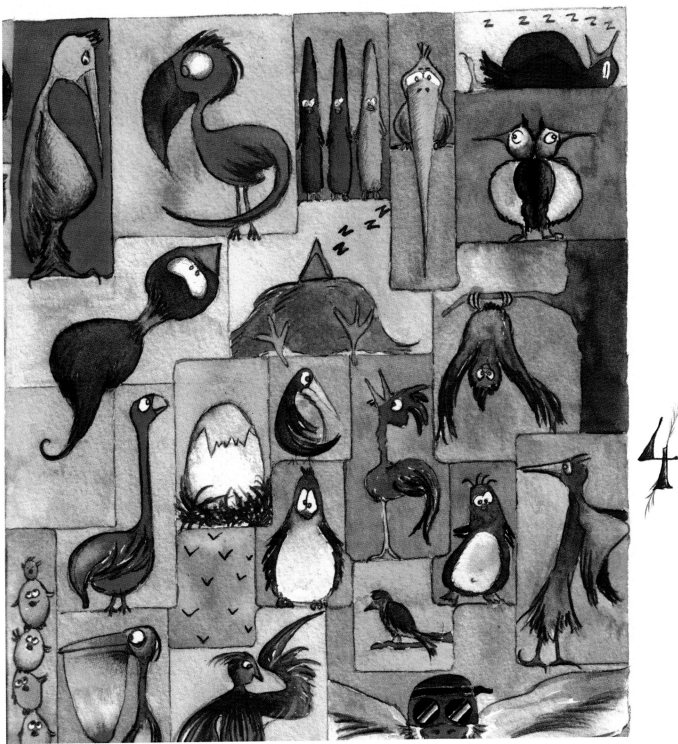

4

Some came in flocks and some came in herds,
Some birds were cool and some birds were nerds.
There were birds with really bedazzling beaks,
Some birds sang beautifully - others made squeaks,
Some birds were tall and others were small,
But the most incredibly beautiful bird of all...

5

Was the Ooch-me noodle bird!
He had feathers of so many different hues –
Purples and pinks and greens and blues!
His head was red and his neck was long,
His wings were wide and shiny and strong.
He lived way up high in the tops of trees,

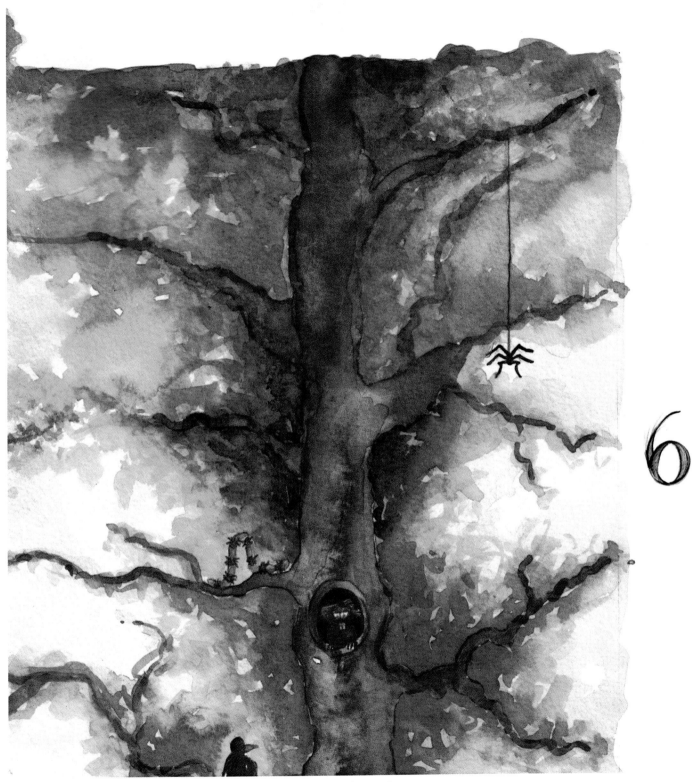

6

So his legs were short and he had no knees
But he had the most magnificent tail,
A tail beside which all others would pale –
Long and fluffy and colorfully bold,
His noodle was quite a sight to behold.

7

As he circled the skies hunting for flies
His noodle would bob up and down.
It allowed him to swoop and dive at will,
He flew through the air with incredible skill.
But down on the ground, the great bird was in trouble –

His noodle was too long for lift-off!
Along he would run on his legs with no knees
Flapping his wings to catch a good breeze –
His noodle would beat up and down, up and down,
And every time that it touched the ground
He screamed, "Ooch-me-noodle, ooch-me-noodle, ooch-me-noodle!"

9

So most of the time he stayed way up high
Living in forests where trees touched the sky.
He built his nests with the greatest of ease

By weaving together the branches of trees.
People like us who live down on the ground
Hardly knew such a bird was around.

But then, not so very long ago,
Along came transport to change the whole show.
Boats and planes and cars and trains –
People conquered mountains, oceans, high plains,
They built new houses wherever they pleased –

And what did they build them with? Why nothing but trees!
Little by little the forests got smaller,
The animals lost their homes.
Places that once were so far away
Were invaded by people every day.

13

For the very first time in the history of man,
The Ooch-me-noodle bird had to live on the land.
His noodle drooped sadly, his wings became dusty,
He could only take off when the wind was gusty,
His pitiful voice echoed all round –

"Ooch-me-noodle, ooch-me-noodle, ooch-me-noodle."
Many of these beautiful birds died of sadness
And some flew into windows in madness.
People began to collect their poor noodles
And add them to flower arrangements.

Then a designer, and I won't name names
Did something of which we should all be ashamed –
Dresses and hats and suits he made
Out of noodles, and then put them all on parade!
Noodles became the latest craze

And in a matter of several days
Tens of thousands of orders arrived
For anything made with a noodle.
Chain stores soon joined in the furor
And people wanted more and more and more.

But these birds died without tails, you see –
And with such short legs and not enough trees
They were doomed, and soon the very last one
Was made into a hat, and then there were none.

People still thought feathers were fantastic
So the designers tried to make them out of plastic –
But they were much too hard and they felt absurd
So there was nothing for it but to kill more birds!
They started with the Peacock and the Dodo and the Squalla
Any bird would do if it had a bit of color.

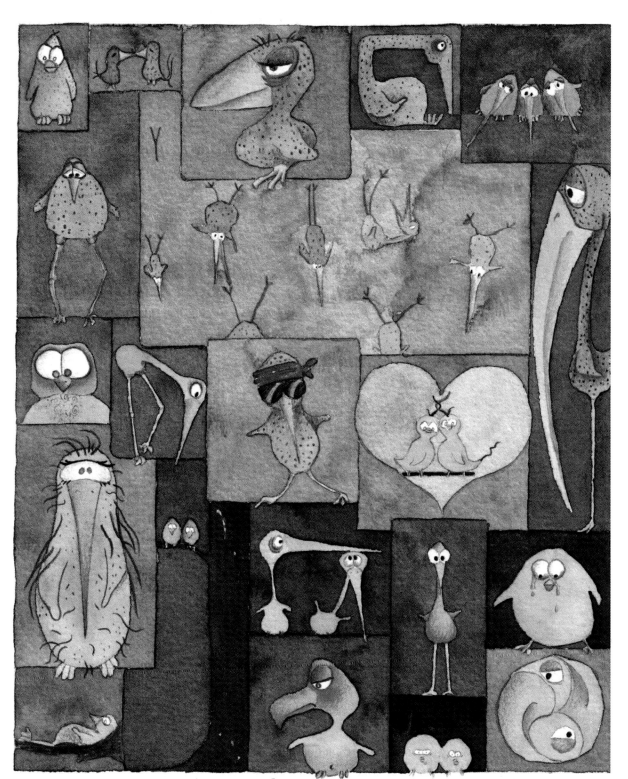

They tried to keep the birds alive and only pick their feathers,
But the poor things froze and fried in all the kinds of weather.
For in a world where there are not enough trees
The hot places get hotter and the cold places freeze.
Red birds were the favorites, and after that came blue-
Soon the only place to see a bird was in the zoo.

20

It wasn't until then that people began to worry,
But it was much too late by the time they were sorry!!
There was one color feather that nobody had wanted,
One type of bird that nobody had hunted –
The brown birds were still alive and hiding in the trees,
And so a law was passed to make them protected species.

Wearing clothes with any feathers was strictly not allowed,
And anyone who did so soon attracted angry crowds.
All those beautiful clothes which from feathers had been made
Were put away in wardrobes to gather dust and fade.
As for the birds – well, for them it was too late,
All but a small handful had already met their fate.

"But Grandpa" I said, feeling quite mad,
"If this is so it means people are bad!
Please tell me it cannot be true that there is nothing we can do.
I want to see pink birds and red birds and blue,
And I want to see Ooch-me-noodle birds, too.
There must be something that can be done -
Surely someone somewhere has saved just one?"

And as we left the park that day
Walking back slowly through the smog and grey,
Grandpa said, "I have heard them say
That one Ooch-me-noodle bird was so brave
He gathered survivors from far and wide

And found a place for them all to hide.
This place is up in the mountains so high
That men cannot walk there and clouds hide the sky.
The birds will probably never come down
As long as men live down here on the ground".

Although I was happy to hear some escaped
I swore I would change things one day.
I would find the Ooch-me-noodle bird tribe
And show them they no longer needed to hide.
We can all live together, there must be a way
To bring the ooch-me-noodle bird back to stay.
Well what do YOU think we can possibly do?
The answer to that is with me and with you.

The Ooch~Me~Noodle Bird

written by Victoria Shaw
illustrated by Joelle Kremers

CEDAR HILL PUBLISHING

The Ooch-Me-Noodle Bird

All illustrations by Joelle Krèmers

Cover Design by Rebecca Hayes

Compiled and edited by Rebecca Hayes

First Edition Spring 2005

Library of Congress Control Number: 2004107711

Published in the United States by
Cedar Hill Publishing
P.O. Box 905
Snowflake, Arizona 85937
http://www.cedarhillpublishing.com

ISBN 1-932373-73-X